Poor Old Polly

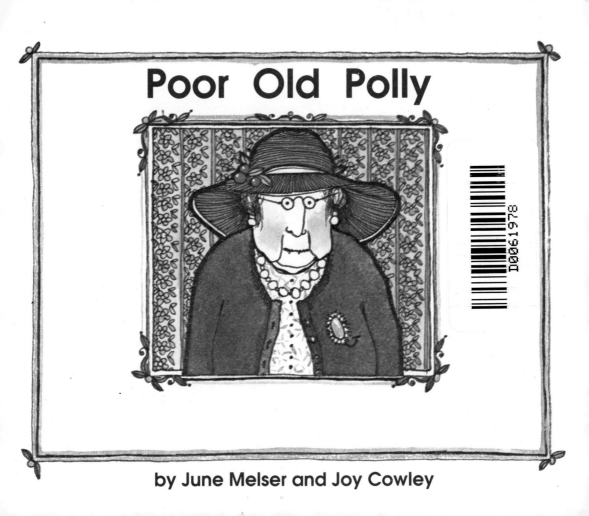

by June Melser and Joy Cowley

Old Polly found a frog;

she swapped it for a dog.

The dog
wouldn't bark;
she swapped it

for a shark.

The shark looked too savage;

she swapped it for a cabbage.
The cabbage was too big;

she swapped it for a pig.

The pig got too bony;

she swapped it for a pony.

The pony wouldn't trot;

she swapped it for a pot.
The pot wouldn't cook;

she swapped it for a book.
The book had no pictures;

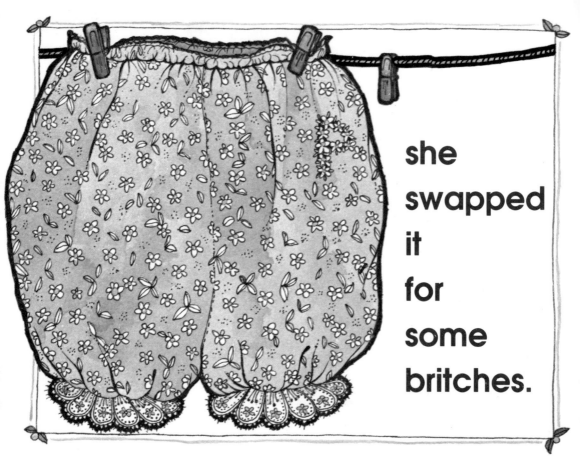

she
swapped
it
for
some
britches.

The britches
were too loose;

13

she swapped them
for a goose.

The goose
gave her
a bite...

and flew off,
out of sight.
Poor old Polly!